THE
SPRING BREAK
FROM THE
BLACK LAGOON®

THE
SPRING BREAK
FROM THE
BLACK LAGOON®

by Mike Thaler
Illustrated by Jared Lee

SCHOLASTIC INC.

In memory of Gene Wooten
—M.T.

To Jana and Jennifer, Daddy's little girls.
—J.L.

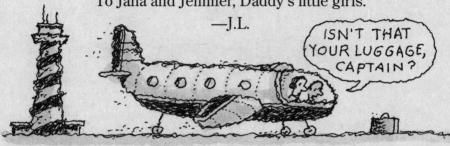

ISN'T THAT YOUR LUGGAGE, CAPTAIN?

Text copyright © 2019 by Mike Thaler
Illustrations copyright © 2019 by Jared Lee

ISBN 978-1-338-24462-5

10 9 8 7 6 5 4 3   20 21 22 23

Printed in the U.S.A.   40

HIPPOPOTAMUS
EXACT SIZE →

CONTENTS

BALD HEAD
↓

ISLAND
↓

CHAPTER 1
SPRING BREAK

It's spring break. That means we get a break from school. No schoolwork or homework.

WHAT TO DO? WHAT TO DO?

WE COULD FEED THE BIRDS.

I already planned out the whole week. I have a pile of comic books. It's going to be a week of superheroes and sleeping late.

Maybe I won't even get out of bed. No stress, no dress, no tests.

"Pack your bag, Hubie!" Mom says.

"Give me a break, I'm on vacation."

"That's right, Hubie, and we're going to Grandma's."

9

CHAPTER 2
A DARK MORNING

"We have a six-thirty flight," Mom says.

"I'll have the whole day to pack," I say.

"Six-thirty a.m."

MOM, EVEN PILOTS DON'T GET UP THAT EARLY.

"There's a 'six-thirty' in the morning, too?"

"Very funny," Mom says.

"I don't want to go. Can't you go without me? I'll be fine, I won't even leave my bed," I beg.

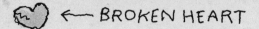
← BROKEN HEART

"Hubie, it would break Grandma's heart if you didn't come. You're her favorite grandson."

HUBIE UP AGAINST THE WALL

"Mom, I'm her *ONLY* grandson."
"More reason to go . . . pack up!"

HAVE YOU SEEN SANTA?

WHO ME?

13

CHAPTER 3
PACK IT UP

First, I pull out my suitcase. I put in all my comic books.

Mom walks into my room. "And what are you doing, young man?" she asks.

"I have to have something to read."

"You can take one for the plane but when we get to Grandma's you're *not* going to be reading comic books in the bedroom the whole time!"

This spring break is going to break me.

CHAPTER 4
A PINCH OF GRANDMA

That night I have a dream. A huge version of Grandma is pinching my cheeks and saying "cute boy, cute boy" over and over again.

SCARED GNAT

The alarm goes off at three a.m.
I blink. It is still dark outside.
How can it look so much like
nighttime if it's supposed to be
the morning?

I make my way to the bathroom.
I comb my teeth and brush my
face. I put my foot in my shirt and
my arms in my pants. Then I go
downstairs to breakfast.

CHAPTER 5
DOGGONE IT

Mom made a lot of food but I'm not hungry. It feels like I just finished dinner.

◊ ←TEAR   ◊ ← RAINDROP

"Mom, what about Tailspin?"

"We're dropping him off with a pet sitter for a few days."

"We can't do that! Look at him—he's crying."

She looks and he is.

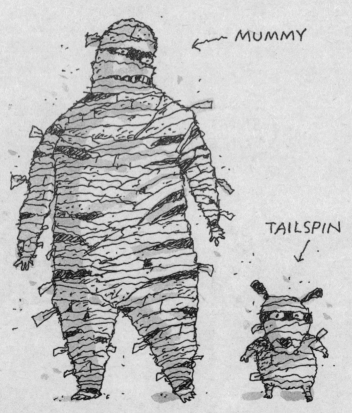

BUG MUMMY

"We can't take him with us. Grandma's allergic to fur."

"We'll shave him. We'll wrap him up like a mummy. Mom, we have to take him!"

MUMMY

TAILSPIN

CHAPTER 6
TAILSPIN TRAVELS WELL

I find a box and put a lot of little holes in it. Then I put Tailspin in it, too. It works fine until we check in at the airport.

"What's in the box?" asks the airport security guard.

HE'S MY BEST FRIEND.

SCRATCH SCRATCH

"It's just my dog. He's small and I need him."

"How so?" asks the guard.

SCRATCH SCRATCH

"It'll break my heart to leave him behind."

"Okay, as long as he doesn't set off the alarm."

He doesn't.

SURE.

CAN YOU SCRATCH MY BACK?

PETER PILOT →

CHAPTER 7
FLYIN' HIGH

Everything is fine on the plane until the flight attendant says, "In the event of a water landing . . ."

OH, GREAT.

"Do planes float, Mom?" I ask. "Don't worry, Hubie. We're flying over the desert."

WHAT ARE YOU DOING?

FLOATING.

I picture a desert landing—having to cross the sand while dying of thirst, calling out "Water, water!"

CAPTAIN, ISN'T THAT THE KID IN 25C?

Then I realize that with one more *s*, the desert would become dessert. That's a place I'd like to land.

I buckle my seat belt around me and Tailspin, and we head up to the sky.

CHAPTER 8
THE VIEW FROM ABOVE

When I look down I can see mountains and fields and forests.

When I look up I can see clouds
and stars. I feel like a superhero.

29

The flight attendant brings me orange juice, tomato juice, ginger ale, and tea. I can't make up my mind.

And lots of pretzels. Only I can't open the little plastic bags. I am still trying when the plane lands.

CHAPTER 9
GRANDMA

BEAR HUG

Grandma runs up and hugs me. *She must have been a wrestler*, I think.

GRANDMA!

"You've grown so much!" exclaims Grandma.

I feel the same size I always am.

Well, at least she didn't pinch my checks, I think.

Just then she grabs hold of both cheeks.

NOT THE CHEEKS!

"What a cute boy! That's my grandson!" she announces to all the passengers in the airport.

After the greeting ritual we head to the parking lot. Grandma rolls the suitcase. I rub my cheeks.

OOPS!

CHAPTER 10
WHEELS

"Which car is yours, Grandma?"
I ask.

"Oh, I don't have a car anymore.
I traded it in for a motorcycle."

Right then we stop in front of a big, shiny, bright red Snarly-Davidson.

CHAPTER 11
HANG ON!

With the bags strapped on either side, Grandma driving, Mom on the back, me in the middle, and Tailspin hanging on for dear life—we roar out of the parking garage.

Luckily, Grandma has helmets for everyone. Except Tailspin.

CHAPTER 12
HOME AWAY FROM HOME

After a whirlwind ride, we pull up in front of Grandma's condo.

"We're here!" she yells.

I open my eyes.

"Fun!" shouts Grandma.

At least we didn't do wheelies, I think.

CHAPTER 13
OUCH IN COUCH

While we're here I have to sleep on the fold-out couch in the living room. It is a contraption of steel springs and metal bars that looks like it was made one hundred years ago.

42.

After the motorcycle ride, I am ready for a nap.

"No way, Hubie!" shouts Grandma. "Put on your bathing suit. We're going swimming!"

45

CHAPTER 14
DIVING RIGHT IN

I learned how to swim for Penny's party, but I never learned how to dive.

"I'll teach you!" shouts Grandma as she leads me up the diving board ladder. Grandma bounces three times and does a perfect swan dive into the deep water.

"Come on, Hubie, it's easy!" she yells while climbing out of the pool.

I try it but I look more like a hurt duck than a swan.

SWIMMING IS EASY.

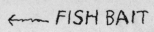

"Good start," says Grandma. "Tomorrow, I'll teach you the somersault."

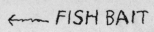

CHAPTER 15
SWEET SCREAMS

That night, Grandma keeps everyone up telling stories about when Mom was a little girl. Finally she unfolds the couch and makes my bed.

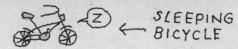

SLEEPING
BICYCLE

"Sweet dreams!" she says, kissing me on the forehead.

When I finally fall asleep, my dreams are anything but sweet.

SLEEPING
BISON

I am on a plane that is plummeting toward Earth. I realize it is heading toward Grandma's swimming pool. It is getting bigger and bigger. Grandma is strapped in next to me.

CHAPTER 16
RIDE OF YOUR LIFE

Grandma wakes me up early for exercise and jogging. Now I know why old people walk bent over. They all must sleep on a fold-out couch from 1914.

"Today is a big day," she says. "We're going to Dizzyland."

The wildest ride is getting there.

"Grandma, do you have a driver's license?"

"I don't think you need one for a motorcycle," she says.

CHAPTER 17

ONE BRAVE GRANNY

Grandma goes on all the rides . . . twice!

The Whirlwind.

"That was fun!" she says.

The Devil's Drop.

"Fun!!" she says.

NICE KITTY→

Lover's Leap.

"Hold on, Hubie!" she says.

It is called an amusement park, but I am not amused.

"Tomorrow, I'll teach you how to skateboard!" Grandma smiles.

CANTALOUPE →

CHAPTER 18
THE MEMORIES WE MADE

I learn a lot of new things during the week.

I learn how to pick a ripe cantaloupe. How to play Mahjong. And how to downshift on a motorcycle.

I also learn a lot about Mom. Every night, Grandma gets out her old leather photo album and we look at pictures from when Mom was a little girl. It is amazing to think of Mom as the same age as me. But Grandma has lots of stories to prove it.

ANTELOPE →

 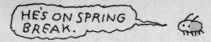

"Life goes fast," sighs Grandma.
And the week goes fast, too.

I am surprised when I have to pack my bag again.

"Already, Mom? Do we have to go so soon?"

"We have to get home, Hubie. School starts back on Monday."

CHAPTER 19

IT'S SO HARD TO SAY GOODBYE

Grandma buys me so many new things: socks, underwear, a Mahjong set—that I can't shut my suitcase. But then Grandma sits on it and I finally get it zipped up.

61

At the airport, Grandma hugs me, Mom, and Tailspin.

We are all a lot closer now.
None of us wants to say goodbye,
and there's a tear in my eye..

On the flight home I don't read my comic book. I gave it to Grandma to keep before I left. I just look out the window as the clouds go by and remember each moment of this amazing spring break.